caillou®

In The Garden

Adaptation of the animated series: Marion Johnson
Illustrations taken from the animated series; adapted by Eric Sévigny

Caillou was playing indoors.
Vroom! vroom! vroom! He raced his toy car around the kitchen.
"Why don't you go outside, Caillou?" Mommy asked.
"There's somebody waiting for you in the garden."

Caillou hurried outside. "Grandpa!" Caillou saw
his Grandpa digging in the garden. "What are
you doing?"
"I'm making a vegetable patch for your mommy,"
Grandpa explained. "Would you like to help?"

"Okay," said Caillou. Digging in the ground looked like fun.
"Do you want to have your own special vegetable to grow?" Grandpa asked.
"Yes!"

"Your special vegetable will be carrots," said Grandpa.
He poured tiny seeds into Caillou's hand.
"But where are the carrots?" asked Caillou.
"First you plant these seeds in the ground," Grandpa
explained. "Then you give them lots of water and wait
for them to grow."

Caillou planted the seeds in holes in the ground.
He watered them with his watering can.
Then he sat down and waited for them to start growing.
"It's not working," Caillou told Grandpa. "No carrots!"
"Oh, you have to wait," Grandpa explained. "It'll take
all summer for the carrots to grow."

Caillou and Grandpa went inside and sat at the kitchen table. Caillou made a drawing of a carrot. Grandpa glued the drawing to a stick.
Now Caillou had a marker for his carrot patch, so he wouldn't forget where he planted his seeds.

Every day Caillou went to check on his carrot patch.
Every day it looked the same.
Finally, Caillou saw something new.
He bent down to take a closer look.
There were green leaves growing!

Caillou waited and waited for his carrots to grow.
It was taking so long!
One day Caillou saw a squirrel digging in the garden.
"No!" cried Caillou. "Those are MY carrots. Shoo!
Shoo! Shoo!"
Caillou chased the squirrel away.

At last, Grandpa said, "I think your carrots are ready
now, Caillou."
But Caillou still didn't see any carrots.
Grandpa said, "Just pull on those leaves."
Caillou grabbed a bunch of leaves and pulled hard.
And out of the ground popped a carrot!

Grandpa and Caillou pulled lots of carrots out of the ground. They took them to Mommy, and she cooked them for dinner.

"I grew these carrots," Caillou said proudly.

"Congratulations, Caillou!" Mommy said. "I think Rosie really likes your carrots."

"What do you think, Caillou?" asked Grandpa.
Caillou looked at the carrots on his plate and took a bite.
"Mmmm!" said Caillou. "These are the best carrots ever!"

Text adapted by Marion Johnson from the scenario of the CAILLOU animated
film series produced by Cookie Jar Entertainment Inc. (©1997 CINAR
Productions (2004) Inc., a subsidiary of Cookie Jar Entertainment Inc.).
All rights reserved.
Original script written by Pascal Lavoie.
Illustrations taken from the animated television series
and adapted by Eric Sévigny.
Art Director: Monique Dupras

The PBS KIDS logo is a registered mark of PBS and is used with permission.

We acknowledge the financial support of the Government of Canada through
the Canada Book Fund for our publishing activities.

Canadian   Patrimoine
Heritage   canadien

We acknowledge the support of the Ministry of Culture and Communications
of Quebec and SODEC for the publication and promotion of this book.

SODEC
Québec

Bibliothèque et Archives nationales du Québec and Library and Archives
Canada cataloguing in publication

Johnson, Marion, 1949-
Caillou in the garden
(Playtime)
For children aged 3 and up.

ISBN 978-2-89450-383-6

1. Vegetable gardening - Juvenile literature. 2. Gardening - Juvenile
literature. I. Sévigny, Eric. II. Cookie Jar Entertainment Inc. III. Title.
IV. Series: Playtime (Montreal, Quebec).

SB324.J63 2005   j635'.04   C2002-941824-0

Legal deposit: 2005